The Mystery of Bloody River
Steven Vagovics

Some of the story information may be lacking due to their mentioning in the previous book episodes of the series.

I.

Honolulu, Hawaii
2 December, 1947

It was another sunny day on Honolulu.

Gilbert Frederich, local businessman, was on his way to work. He was a middle-aged man with brown hair, a fattish figure and green eyes who owned one of the biggest companies involved with cash loan services in Honolulu called SUNBEAM FINANCES. It was known that Gilbert was a rich man. After all, his company was making thousands of dollars in profit every day and still growing. As he was walking through Foster Botanic Garden, he saw a few young children who were on a school trip with their teacher. They spread joy all around the park and Gilbert looked at the teacher. She was an older woman with blond hair, blue eyes and a fit figure.

Gilbert started talking with her.

- Look at them little children! How much joy they're having! Isn't it just amazing?

Teacher replied with a smile on her face.

- Yes, I agree. They are my pride. I see a great potential in each one of them. It doesn't matter that they are only nine years old. I can envision the intelligent and well-behaved adults they are about to become.

Gilbert nodded his head.

- It's just fascinating how one can develop so rapidly during so little time. Suddenly, it stops and you remain almost exactly the same for so long.
- Perhaps, that's true.

After a moment of silence, the teacher realised something and asked with curiosity.

- Wait a minute. Aren't you that rich man, Gilbert? I've seen you so many times on television already!

Gilbert smiled and replied.

- Yes, that's me.

The teacher continued.

- Just a moment. I think I saw a report just this morning about you.

Suddenly, Gilbert was surprised.

- What was it about?
- It was a report about some changes that are about to happen in your company.

Gilbert was even more suprised and wondered.

- I don't know anything about it. Did they mention precisely what changes are about to happen?
- No, they didn't. At least, I don't remember anything.
- I see.

Gilbert became slightly nervous.

- I'll keep on walking then. I have to go there to find out about it. See you later.
- Bye.

Gilbert walked on through the park and couldn't think of a single reason to explain what the teacher had talked about. He started to rush. After a few minutes, he reached the company and entered. A lot of people were panicking inside the building and Gilbert was terrified. When he walked into his office, Joe Pentham appeared . It was Gilbert's business partner who ran the company with him. He was a tall person with black hair and a thin figure who was just as old as Gilbert. He asked with fear.

- Gil, have you heard the news yet?

Gilbert answered with insecurity.

- No, I haven't. What the hell happened? I don't like this. Why are so many people here?

Joe replied.

- Gil, this is serious. Do you remember that new company Calico?
- Yes, I do. They were about to go bankrupt just a few days ago. What about them?

Joe got a bit upset and explained.

- Listen, Gil. I don't know how to tell you this but... They are taking over!

Gilbert looked at Joe with surprise. He didn't understand.

- What do you mean they are taking over?

Joe started shouting.

- They are taking over! Literally! They ran a huge campaign about their cash loan services which provided offers we just can't compete with! Most of our clients switched over to the them, leaving us hopeless. We're screwed!

Gilbert thought for a little.

- Wait, something's weird here. Our clients signed a clear contract which stated their liability with us until their loan is paid off. How could they just switch to Calico? I can't accept that.
- It's a complicated situation. They found a loophole in our contract papers and took advantage of it right away! This resulted in several benefits for people who switched. Additionally, they found a way to do it behind our backs!

Gilbert started pacing around the office nervously.

- This is not good. Oh, this is bad! This is bad! So what's next?

- Our company is getting shut down and we're going to lose a lot of money.
- How much money are we talking about?

Joe grabbed a file and gave it to Gilbert without words.

- Take a look at this. It's all stated here. I recommend you sit down, Gil.

Gilbert sat down and opened the file. His expression turned to fury. Joe tried to calm him down.

- I'm so sorry, Gil. I know it's a lot of money but I'm sure you'll be able to handle it well.

Gilbert remained silent.

- Gil, are you all right? Is it more than you expected? Gil?

Gilbert stood up. He began to speak with anger.

- Do you... Do you really want to know?

Joe replied with worry.

- Yes, tell me.
- All right then. I'll tell you.

Gilbert grabbed a lamp which was placed on his desk and threw it at the door fiercely. The lamp smashed to pieces. Afterwards, he shouted.

- It's almost everything I've got! What the bloody hell? For goodness' sake, how could you let something like this happen? This is unbelievable!

Joe replied with fear.

- Gil, look, I'm sorry! There was basically nothing I could do about it! Even if I could do something, I don't have all the rights that you do!

Gilbert slowly sat down again and stated in a quiet, angry voice.

- Get out of my office right now. I need to be alone.
- But Gil!
- Right... now!

Joe left the office and Gilbert sat in his chair for a moment, thinking about the whole situation. After a moment, he grabbed his bag and left the building.

A few hours later, he came home where his wife was waiting for him. Her name was Claudia. She was a tall, blue-eyed woman with long black hair and a thin figure. When Gilbert opened the door, Claudia was talking on a telephone.

- What do you mean by that? Oh, I see.

Gilbert became uncomfortable when he heard these words. He thought that the conversation might have been about him. Claudia hung up the telephone and spoke to Gilbert.

- Gilbert, I've just found out about what happened today.

Gilbert got upset. Claudia continued talking.

- Look, Gilbert. It's okay. We can handle this. We still have enough money to start something new.
- I'm not sure about that, honey.
- Why not?
- Do you know how big of a loss this situation has brought to us? Calico simply took over! All of my clients are there now. I have nothing to work with because of that!
- Let's just hope we can figure this out, Gilbert.
- But how, Claudia? We have nothing! No money, no business anymore and we can probably say goodbye to this house!

Gilbert became very angry and strongly punched the wall. Claudia was shocked. After a little while, Gilbert calmed down and said.

- I need to go out. I just... can't stand here without doing anything. I'm sorry, honey.

Gilbert quickly opened the door and ran away. Claudia was trying to reason with him but without success. Gilbert was gone.

II.

Honolulu, Hawaii
3 December, 1947

The next morning, Claudia woke up and Gilbert was still not back. Full of fear, she went to the kitchen, turned on the radio, made herself a cup of coffee and sat at the table with the newspaper. The news broadcast started.

- *Good morning Honolulu. In today's newsflash – riot in Jerusalem caused by the United Nations, three women escapees from Honolulu on their visit, a man found by the river.*

Claudia was even more terrified. With a cup of coffee in her hands, she listened with the darkest images in her mind already. The news continued.

- *The riot in Jerusalem occured yesterday when the Arab Higher Committee declared a three-day strike and public protest against the United Nations plan to create two states – one Jewish and one Arab in Palestine, according to the 1947 UN Partition Plan. Our reporters have just been sent to Palestine to bring you more information about the situation. Three Australian girls who evaded US police inHonolulu while being deported from America wait for another trial for their crimes. A body has been reported this morning lying by the Anahulu River in the Haleiwa Ali'i Beach Park. According to police, two women saw the man lying on the ground in the distance. We're currently patiently waiting for confirmation of whether the man is dead or just unconscious.*

Claudia's hands were shaking as she reached up for the telephone which was near the table. She dialed Joe's phone number and when he picked up, she started talking in great fear.

- Joe, what did you do?

Joe replied with insecurity.

- What? Who am I talking with?
- It's me, you little brat! What did you do?
- I don't know what you're talking about.
- Bastard!

Claudia hung up and started crying.

III.

The Police Station
3 December, 1947

At the police station, Lieutenant Phil More held a press conference about the found body. Questions were coming across the entire room.

- Lieutenant More, Honolulu Paper repoter Mandy Simmons speaking.Do you know whether the found man is just unconscious or dead already?
- Our police officers should be here any minute now. Just be patient. In either case, this situation has to be investigated.

- Lieutenant Phil More, Waikiki News reporter Liz Anderson.What's the investigation going to look like?
- That's a good question, Missus Anderson. It depends on whether the found man is dead or just unconscious. If it turns out that the man is just unconscious, our police officers will interrogate him when he regains consciousness. That's all I can say at the moment.

Lieutenant More heard a car pulling up to the building. With a sigh of relief, he stated.

- Oh, it sounds like our police officers are here.

After a short moment, two police officers entered the room and spoke.

- Lieutenant, could we speak with you for a moment?
- Of course. Just a minute, folks.

Lieutenant More went out of the room along with the police officers. They closed the door on their way out and started talking in the corridor.

- Lieutenant, the man is dead. It appears that a murder occured last night.
- Hmm... That's what I thought, to be honest. I mean seriously, unconscious body? Those reporters nowadays are quite delusional.What a bunch of laughable brats! So, who is the man?
- His name is, or rather was, Gilbert Frederich.

Lieutenant More was surprised as this name sounded familiar to him.

- That Gilbert Frederich? Really? He was quite a popular businessman in Honolulu. How come nobody recognised him?
- That's not such a hard question to answer, Lieutenant. He was found facedown. Also, the entire body was wet. It looks like someone either threw it into the river and it washed ashore or someone pulled the body from the water.

- Oh, I see. Call detective Herbie Fox, then. He's the only reliable person I can think of right now. I'm going to finish the press conference.
- Yes, sir.

Lieutenant More returned to the press conference. He continued speaking.

- All right, I have some new information about the body. It seems like a murder was committed during the night.

The journalists slightly panicked and started asking futher questions.

- Mary Smith, Hawaii Today reporter.Who is the murdered man?
- His name was Gilbert Frederich. Yes, we're talking about the popular businessman.

Everyone in the room was shocked. Lieutenant More tried to calm the journalists down.

- Look! Everything is under control! We're going to do our best to find out who committed this terrible crime and that person will be punished! I would like to ask you to remain calm.

- Jane Foster, Aloha Paper.Do you think our security is too loose?

When the lieutenant heard these words, he became angry.

- For crying out loud! What kind of a question is that supposed to be? You know what? I've had enough! This press conference is over! Thank you for coming!

The journalists were surprised and their shouting accompanied the lieutenant's walking out of the room. Afterwards, the lieutenant entered his office with frustration. He sat down at his desk and covered his face with his palms. After a moment, detective Herbie Fox appeared in the office.

- I heard you wanted to see me, Lieutenant.
- Oh, Fox! I wouldn't ever say that seeing you would brighten up my day!
- How delightful, Lieutenant. I think we should slow down, though. You're making me feel uncomfortable!

Lieutenant More laughed.

- Fox, I would advise you to stop making jokes. We have a serious case on our hands and this one is somehow... everywhere.
- What do you mean, Lieutenant?
- Gee, don't you have a radio, Fox? I woke up this morning and it was the first thing I heard. A body was found by the Anahulu River. Those idiots even thought that the poor man was just unconscious. It's one of the stupidest things I've ever heard on the radio. For crying out loud!

The lieutenant grew angry again and Herbie tried to calm him down.

- Calm down, Lieutenant. You can be glad that you haven't seen The Jack Eigen Show on television. I think that you would have a heart attack by listening to the things that guy says!
- Not funny, Fox! Don't try to be a comedian!
- I'm sorry, Lieutenant.

A few seconds of rather awkward silence occured in the office. Shortly after, the lieutenant started talking in a serious manner.

- Anyway, the man who was found is Gilbert Frederich. Have you heard of him? I bet you have, Fox.
- Oh yeah, that businessman. He tried to look like a good and generous fella but deep inside, I think he might have been even more crooked than the others.
- Perhaps. I don't know much about the guy but I met him once. His business partner got into trouble once and he came here to bail him out of the prison cell.

Lieutenant More grew silent for a moment and Herbie asked.

- So, where is Albert Fringe?
- Oh, about that. I'm so busy and stressed out that I haven't even found the time to assign you a partner. Please, Fox, do me a favor and call him. This is his number.

Lieutenant More opened a drawer and took out a piece of paper with Albert Fringe's telephone number on it. He gave it to Herbie. Herbie left the office and went straight to the nearest telephone booth. He dialed the number and a female voice answered.

- This is the operator.It seems the number you are trying to reach is unavailable at the moment.

Herbie waited for a minute and tried to dial the number again. The female voice repeated the message.

- This is the operator. It seems the number you are trying to reach is unavailable at the moment.

Herbie thought to himself.

- Where is Albie? It looks like he's not home right now.

When Herbie tried to dial the number for the third time with the same results, he gave up. He went back to the lieutenant's office. The lieutenant was having a telephone conversation.

- Yes, it's about that new case. Found body by the river. We need another detective to join Herbie Fox. What about Albert Fringe? Is he available?

A few seconds later, the lieutenant continued.

- I see. So what is his name?

...
- Gerald Horwitz. Is he good?

...
- We'll see about that. Thank you and have a nice day.

Lieutenant More hung up and told Herbie.

- Fox, Fringe is on a vacation. You have a new partner.

Herbie got slightly angry.

- I don't like this, Lieutenant. Just a few months ago, you assigned me a youngster who was completely unknown to me and now you're trying to pull it off again with someone else?
- Fox, don't be such a prima donna! Just because you worked alone for so many years doesn't mean you don't need a partner! I'm sorry about that, Fox. Things change. You know, you're not that young anymore! Gerald Horwitz will be fine.

Suddenly, a tall man came to the office. He had short black hair and a strong figure.

- Did you just say my name? Gerald Horwitz, pleased to meet you... Herbie? Harold? Hercules?

Gerald laughed out loudbut both Herbie and More remained silent. Gerald continued.

- Come on, you two old rascals! Give me a little smile!

19

Herbie was a little uncomfortable and didn't say a word. Lieutenant More spoke with anger.

- Horwitz! What kind of an introduction is that supposed to be? How old are you, anyway?

Gerald replied.

- I'm fifty-five years young, Lieutenant.

Lieutenant More shook his head in despair without a reply. Herbie stated.

- No offense, Mister Horwitz, but you're acting like a moron!

Gerald laughed out loud and placed his hand on Herbie's shoulder.

- Good joke, Foxy! I think I'm gonna call you foxy lady! What a name! Sounds like a great rock and roll song!

Herbie became angry, too.

- Enough, Horwitz! Lieutenant, are you serious? Is this really the guy I'm supposed to work with? Even I don't find it funny. I want someone else as my partner!

Lieutenant More shouted.

- Listen! You both are making me angry! Horwitz, stop acting like a child! Fox, try to understand the pressure I'm under and cooperate already! Now, you two will go to the crime scene and start investigating! You probably don't realise that you're detectives and not stand-up comedians! A man was killed yesterday! Get out of my office and go to Haleiwa Ali'i Beach Park! And Horwitz, don't try to make fun of me or I'll make such a great fun of you that you'll cry! Do you understand?

Gerald replied with a serious manner.

- Yes, sir.
- Good! Get out of my face! Both of you!

Herbie and Gerald left the lieutenant's office and went to the car.

- Mister Horwitz, you're the driver!
- All right.

As they were driving, they had a conversation. Gerald started.

- So Herbie, what do you know about this case?

Herbie sighed and replied with a lower tone of voice.

- Mister Horwitz, I don't want to be rude but I don't know that much and it's because of you! Why did you have to act like a little child in the lieutenant's office?

He's a serious man who hates when someone doesn't treat him with the respect he deserves. The same applies to me, you Horwi lady!

- Come on, Herbie. Why are you all so serious? Have a little laught.
- I have no reason to laugh right now, Mister Horwitz. Maybe I would if you were at least funny.
- Don't be so mean, Herbie! You're hurting my feelings!
- Please, if you don't have anything interesting to say, stay quiet.
- You know I'm not going to do that.
- You're such a dork, Horwitz! Who are you, anyway? I can't even remember hearing your name at all! Tell me something about yourself.
- My name is Gerald and I'm a detective.
- Anything more to add, you baby?
- I don't think so.
- Fine. Just drive then and for the goodness's sake, be quiet!

Herbie was surprised when Gerald remained silent. A few minutes later, they arrived at the Ali'i Beach Park.

IV.

The Crime Scene
Ali'i Beach Park

3 December, 1947

Herbie and Gerald got out of the car. The beach park was surrounded by journalists and police officers. Herbie thought to himself.

- Wow, this is probably one of the most hyped cases I've ever encountered!

Gerald took advantage of the journalists and started showboating in front of them. Herbie ignored him and noticed Officer Blake standing nearby. He went to talk with him.

- Officer Blake! Good seeing you here!
- Hello, Mister Fox! Seems just like yesterday when that daisy case got reported!
- Quite frankly, yes! It was just a few months ago. I think it happened in March if I remember correctly.
- I guess. Anyway, who is your partner now?
- Gerald Horwitz is his name. To be honest with you, he looks like an idiot!
- That's strange. That name doesn't ring any bells for me.

- That's exactly what I thought, too! Who is this guy supposed to be?
- Well, he's probably not so bad. Not everyone can be assigned to such a great detective as you are, Mister Fox!
- Thank you for the kind words, Officer Blake. I'm not sure about that, though. Could you tell me anything more about the case, Officer? This Horwitz guy made the lieutenant so angry he didn't even tell me that much.
- Angry? What did he do?
- You know, I didn't say that he looks like an idiot for no reason, Officer. When he came to the office, he was just laughing and making fun of us both - me and the lieutenant. The poor lieutenant was in despair already and then this guy appeared.
- I understand that. Phil More can be pretty moody sometimes. No wonder he made him angry. Nevertheless, I think you might know that the victim was Gilbert Frederich. He was a famous businessman who owned a company called Sunbeam Finances. I'm not sure whether you heard the news or not. It was just yesterday. A rivalry company called Calico took Sunbeam Finances over and caused a bankrupcy.

Herbie thought for a minute.

- That's very interesting. Thinking about it... isn't it possible that he committed... suicide?

- Good question, Mister Fox. It's not impossible. If that's true, the remaining question would be how. I guess the body needs to be analyzed for further clues.
- Of course, Officer Blake. Talking about analysis, have you seen Mister Marston?
- Yes, of course. He's over there by the blue kiosk.
- Thank you, Officer Blake. I'm afraid I have to leave you now.
- All right, Mister Fox. Take care.
- See you, Officer.

Herbie crossed the police line and bent down to the body. When he saw that Gerald was not by his side, he thought to himself.

- Where is that Horwitz guy? I'm afraid there will be a lot of trouble because of that chump.

Herbie observed the body. First, he looked at Gilbert Frederich's head. He noticed the black eye.

- Hmm, a black eye? He was either in a fight somewhere or someone beat him up pretty bad.

He moved on to the pockets of Gilbert's coat. As he was grabbing them from outside the coat, he grappled with his wallet and finally pulled it out. He found a sum of a hundred dollars in it and a Sunbeam Finances business card. Apart from that, there was a picture of him and Claudia inside.

- Let's see. I remember this woman's face from somewhere. If I'm correct, this woman is his wife.

Herbie put the picture inside his coat pocket and continued searching Gilbert's pockets. Apart from the keys from his home, he couldn't find anything.

A few moments later, Dean Marston came to Herbie and spoke to him.

- Mister Fox!

Herbie stood up and replied.

- Mister Marston! I was just about to come and talk to you! What are your observations so far about the body?
- To be honest, this case appears to be bizarre.

Herbie was surprised and asked curiously.

- Why?

Marston bent down to the body and started explaining.

- You see, the body appears to have several wounds on it. It seems like the victim was punched by somebody. I find it strange that the body washed ashore. What is it doing here? You know, the only reasonable explanation would be someone pulling it out the body out of the water. I would even say that it could be suicide. But still, it doesn't make sense, I guess.

Herbie thought for a minute.

- Mister Marston, I think we have an interesting case in our hands. Have you heard anything about Gilbert Frederich in the news recently?
- Yes, I have. Haven't you?
- No, I haven't.
- You see, the main reason why I think it may be suicide is because of what happened to this man.

Herbie grew curious.

- What happened, then?
- Gilbert Frederich owned a cash loan services company called Sunbeam Finances. I think you're aware of that, am I correct?
- Yes, how couldn't I be? That company was so heavily promoted just a few months ago. Everywhere I went, there were flyers about him and the company.
- Yes, that's correct. Something happened just yesterday to the company. Does the name Calico ring any bells for you?
- I think I've heard about it somewhere.
- It's a rival company to Sunbeam Finances. Well... it was.
- Did they go bankrupt?

- Hmm, no. Calico took over the market. On the other hand, Sunbeam Finances did go bankrupt, indeed!
- How could something like that happen?
- If I remember correctly, Calico took over all the clients that Sunbeam Finances had somehow. Strange, I know. But business can be sometimes harsh and strange.
- That's true, Mister Marston. Have you heard anything about his wife Claudia?
- Let me think, Mister Fox. I remember her appearing on the radio a few times.

Marston tried to remember something he had heard about Claudia Frederich but he could only come up with one thing.

- Mister Fox, I can't remember much, just this: I think she mentioned on one show that she and Gilbert can't have children.
- That sounds interesting. Maybe it had something to do with his death, don't you think?
- Nothing's impossible, Mister Fox.

A few moments later, Gerald appeared.

- Herbie, why are you so modest, rascal? I've just had an interview with about five of the journalists here. You can be grateful, Herbie. If I wasn't here, they would surround you instead of me.
- Really, Horwitz? What did you tell them when you know even less about the case than I do right now?

- I have my ways, Herbie. Come on, trust me. Have a little faith in me, rascal! Who is this nice guy?
- This is mister Dean Marston. He performs autopsies at the police station.

Gerald and Marston shook hands.

- Nice to meet you, Mister Marston. My name is Gerald Horwitz. Your job is awesome! Observing dead bodies... you must be a tough fella!

Marston smiled and replied.

- Thank you, Mister Horwitz. I'm pleased to meet you, too!

Herbie joined the conversation.

- Well, at least you dealt with those journalists, Horwitz. Also, it's nice to know that you have some respect for Mister Marston. Anyway, Mister Marston, who do you think would be the best to visit first for the investigation?
- I would say Gilbert's wife. She was probably the most important person to Gilbert, I suppose.
- Horwitz, do me a favor. You heard Mister Marston. Go and find out the address of a woman called Claudia Frederich, will you?

Gerald stated.

- Herbie, you look so charming when you give commands, rascal! All right, I'll go and get it for you.
- Good, Horwitz. Stop with the jokes already!
- Yeah, yeah, Herbie.

Gerald went to talk with the officers to find out Claudia's address. Meanwhile, Marston and Herbie continued talking.

- That guy gives me headaches already, Mister Marston.
- Oh, come on, Mister Fox. He's just immature, that's all. I suppose you can be glad that someone doesn't take himself so seriously. I think it's a nice change.
- I was hoping for that young fella, Albert Fringe. I found him to be a good partner. A bit quiet, but that's how I like it, to be honest.
- And where is he, Mister Fox?
- Apparently, he's on a vacation right now.
- I see.Where did he go?
- I don't know, Mister Marston. I just hope that this Horwitz guy won't cause any trouble. His first impression wasn't very good, you know.
- Don't you worry, Mister Fox. I'm sure it'll be fine.
- I hope you are right, Mister Marston.

A few seconds later, Gerald came back with the address.

- Here it is, Herbie. The address of Claudia Frederich.

- All right, thank you, Horwitz. You're driving. See you around, Mister Marston.
- Come to my office tomorrow, Mister Fox. I'll have the analysis for you.
- Sure thing, Mister Marston. Goodbye.
- Goodbye.

Gerald said goodbye to Marston, too.

- Bye, you awesome toughie!

Marston laughed quietly and replied.

- See you around, Mister Horwitz.

Herbie and Gerald got into the car, leaving the crime scene.

V.

Claudia Frederich
3 December, 1947

A few minutes later, Herbie and Gerald arrived at the house of Gilbert Frederich. They got out of the car and knocked on the door. Eventually, Claudia opened it.

- Detective Herbie Fox. Claudia Frederich?

Claudia replied with fright.

- Yes. Yes, that's me. What do you want?
- We're investigating the murder of your husband, Gilbert.
- I see. This is probably not the right time but come on in.

Herbie and Gerald entered the house.

- I'm just going to get you a cup of coffee, detectives. Sit down on the sofa in the living room.

When they entered the living room, there was a man sitting on the sofa. It was Joe Pentham, Gilbert's business partner. He spoke to the detectives.

- Greetings, detectives.

Herbie was surprised and asked.

- Who are you?

Joe replied.

- My name is Joe Pentham. Together with Gilbert
  Frederich, I ran a company called Sunbeam Finances.
- Detective Herbie Fox. This is my partner, Gerald
  Horwitz.
- Pleased to meet you, detective Fox.

Claudia came inwith two cups of coffee in her hands.

- I hope you don't mind. My friend Joe has just came to
  visit me.

Herbie replied.

- It's all right, missis Frederich. Besides, we don't have
  to visit Joe separately now, I suppose.

Claudia put one cup of coffe on the table. She placed it in
front of Herbie. She kept the second one in her hands and
started drinking softly. Suddenly, Gerald shouted.

- Where is my cup of coffee? I thought the other one
  was for me!

Herbie looked at Gerald with anger.Claudia was surprised and
replied.

- Ex... Excuse me? Why are you shouting at me?

Gerald shouted even loudlier.

- I want coffee! Now!

Claudia got annoyed and stated with antipathy.

- Just a minute, detective.

Claudia went to the kitchen. Joe started speaking.

- That was quite rude, detective!

Gerald replied with a shout.

- Shut up!

Herbie told Gerald with great anger.

- What the hell are you doing, Horwitz? Are you out of your mind?

Gerald remained silent. Joe stood up and went to the kitchen. Herbie continued talking.

- Horwitz, change your behavior immediately! You're nothing but trouble!

Suddenly, Herbie heard an argument coming from the kitchen. He became curious.

- Can you hear that, Horwitz? Sounds like those two are arguing about something in the kitchen!

Herbie tried hard to distinguish the words, but he wasn't able to. After a while, they both returned from the kitchen. Claudia gave Gerald a cup of coffee. Herbie asked a question.

-    Have you just been arguing back there?

They both smiled and replied to Herbie.

-    What? Oh, no, no...

Joe continued.

-    We were just... discussing something. No argument or anything like that.

Herbie was suspicious and stated.

-    All right then. Sit down. Both of you. I would like to start.

Claudia and Joe sat down. Herbie continued after he pulled out his pen and a notebook. Gerald started drinking.

-    Usually, I would leave the writing to you, Mister Horwitz. However, I don't think it's a good idea. Anyway, missis Frederich, tell me exactly what happened yesterday.

Claudia sighed and started talking.

- It's... really difficult for me to talk about it right now. Joe went to work early in the morning and returned much sooner than usual. When he got home, he was very nervous and told me what happened to the company. I didn't know what to say. He said he was going to take a walk and he didn't come home all night.

Claudia was upset and her mood was getting worse. Herbie asked further.

- Can you think of any possible places where Gilbert could have gone?
- Let me think. He liked hanging out in the Lopez Hills Bar. Sometimes, he went out bowling with some of his colleagues. I'm sorry, I really don't know.
- I see. Well, nevermind. How was your marriage with Gilbert? Were you a happy couple?
- Of course we were. Gilbert was a really nice and generous man. I loved him so much...

Claudia started wiping tears off her face. Suddenly, Gerald spoke.

- Whoa! Sorry lady but this coffee tastes like murder! Get it? Murder? But seriously, horrible!

Herbie replied in anger.

- Horwitz! I swear, one more stupid sentence from you and I'll file a complaint!

Joe supported Herbie by adding his two cents.

- Why are you acting like such a jerk? I'm no one to judge you but you really look like an idiot! And Claudia... just stop that!

Claudia looked at Joe with surprise and responded with tears in her eyes.

- What are you trying to say, Joe?

Joe started shouting.

- Come on, don't pretend that you're such an innocent woman! You only married Gilbert for his money!

Claudia cried even more and stated.

- Why are you shouting, Joe? You're hurting me!

Joe continued.

- Yes, just keep your little theater going, Claudia! I'm sick of you!

Herbie shouted, too.

- Enough already! You! Joe! Can't you see that this poor woman is in tears? I'm no one to judge the situation yet but that's not very nice of you! Come on, it's your turn then! Tell me about the company!

Joe calmed down a little and started.

- I met Gilbert in college. We became best friends and we wanted to start our own business. Basically, any business. One day, my family fell into debt. Our bills were overdue and my mother did something very dangerous to keep our home. She borrowed money from a loan shark. A few months passed and we still weren't able to pay our debt. I remember it like it happened yesterday. I was only nineteen at the time. I came home and my mother was nowhere to be seen. She was killed.

Joe became very upset as he continued.

- That day, I swore to my mother's grave. I gave her my honest vow that I wouldn't let this happen to other poor families. Gilbert and I started to work at the local restaurant as waiters. We wanted to earn as much money as possible to start a cash loan business. Luckily, we were successful. That's how Sunbeam Finances was formed.

Herbie claimed.

- That's a very sad story, Mister Joe. Tell me, what happened to the company just a few days ago?

Joe replied.

- A few months ago, a new company started to provide cash loan services. This company is called Calico. Martin Kipp is the founder. He comes from a very rich family. His promises were big. A new modern cash loan service with zero risk for the clients. I don't know how Kipp is able to do what he does. His offers are really extraordinary. If we wanted to try the same methods in our company, we would go bankrupt in just a few days. Anyway, you probably know where I'm heading. Our company simply couldn't match the standards of Calico. It all ended when Kipp offered our clients a switch to Calico for no extra fees, whatsoever. He was successful. We didn't even know what was going on and suddenly, we had no clients! I was thinking about a lawsuit with Calico but it would be a very bad idea. We have no chance against his lawyers. He's too powerful.

Herbie asked further.

- Although it does indeed make sense, I think it's a bit strange. Did Gilbert lose all of his money?

Claudia replied.

- Yes, detective.

Herbie wondered.

- But how?

Joe tried to answer Herbie's question.

- It's... quite difficult to explain, detective. Our financal system was, more or less, a house of cards. When Kipp took over our clients, their loans remained our debts.

Herbie tried to figure it out but he was still not sure.

- I'm sorry, Mister Joe. I still feel like there's something missing. I've heard about Gilbert Frederich before. He was quite famous and it has been said that he was wealthy.

Joe claimed.

- That may be true, detective.

Herbie got suspicious.

- Excuse me, Joe. Are you trying to tell me that you don't know whether that statement was true? You said that you were best friends just a few minutes ago!

Joe was a little nervous already and became uncomfortable.

- Yes... I mean, no. Listen, Gilbert was indeed a rich man. The situation with Calico got out of control and it's very complicated to explain why Gilbert lost his money.

Joe stood up and grabbed his coat.

- Excuse me, detectives. I would rather go now, if you don't mind.

Herbie got confused and replied.

- Well, I think that's everything I need to know for now. Although I have to say, Mister Joe, this may not be the end of our conversation!

Joe replied with a fright.

- All right, detective. See you around. Bye, Claudia.

Joe left the house. Herbie continued the interrogation with Claudia. Even though she still had tears on her face, she had stopped crying.

- So, Missus Frederich. I'm glad to see you're not crying anymore. I would like to excuse my partner for making a scene earlier. He feels sorry about it. Right, Horwitz?

Herbie looked at Gerald with anger. Gerald replied with insecurity.

- Yes, Herbie. I'm sorry, Claudia.

Claudia responded.

- Don't worry about it, detective. At least you were honest about my coffee.

Gerald remained silent and Herbie continued.

- All right, let's move on, missis Frederich. I'm curious. Why was Joe visiting you right now?

Claudia replied.

- We wanted to talk about what happened to Sunbeam Finances. It's unfortunate but I need help. We have some unpaid bills and I'm unemployed.

Herbie thought about it for a few seconds and responded.

- I see. But one thing... how could Joe not lose his money from the bankruptcy?

Claudia claimed.

- That's an easy question, detective. It may sound unbelievable but being a manager at Sunbeam Finances wasn't his only employment.

Herbie got surprised.

- Really? What's his second employment?

Claudia responded.

- He's also an executive manager at Ride-O-Mobil company. They sell used vehicles.

Herbie was even more surprised.

- Is that so? Did Gilbert know about it? Besides, why didn't Joe lend some money to Gilbert? He had enough to do that, I suppose.
- I don't know whether Gilbert knew about it. Joe likes to have some secrets. About the money, I think that Joe would lend him some. He knows the best what it means to experience poverty. I really can't tell. Either way, me and Gilbert never talked about Ride-O-Mobil together.
- I understand. There's one thing that concerns me, missis Frederich. My friend heard a radio show in which you appeared as a guest. He told me that you stated how you can't have children with Gilbert. What can you tell me about that?

Claudia was surprised.

- I honestly don't know what you're talking about, detective.

Herbie grew suspicious and replied.

- Are you sure, missis Frederich? Don't lie to me!

Claudia became terrified and responded.

- I'm being honest, detective! Please believe me!

Herbie stated.

- All right, missis Frederich. I believe you. I think we're finished for now. Did Gilbert have any relatives living nearby?

Claudia thought for a minute.

- Yes. You can either visit Gilbert's brother or his sister.

Herbie replied.

- Good. Could you please give me their addresses?

Herbie gave his pen and notebook to Claudia. She claimed.

- Of course, here they are.

She wrote the addresses in the notebook and returned it to Herbie. He stood up from the sofa and went to the door with Gerald.

- Thank you, missis Frederich. Take care. Horwitz, let's go.

They left the house and got into the car. Herbie told Gerald.

- You know what, Horwitz? I've had enough for today. Take me home, please. I'll give you directions.

- Ok, Herbie. What terrible coffee back there, huh? I would arrest her just for that taste.
- Horwitz, please... I have a headache already.

Claudia was looking out of the window. When they were gone, she picked up the phone and dialed.

- Hey! It's me!
  ...
  Me! Claudia, you moron!
  ...
  You don't say! Listen, they have already been here.
  ...
  Yes, exactly! You should take care of yourself.
  ...
  Why are you asking me? I'm not the one to tell.
  ...

Suddenly, someone rang the doorbell.

- Oh, I have to go now. Someone's here.

She hung up the telephone and went to open the door.

VI.

Herbie's Apartment
3 December, 1947

A few minutes passed and Herbie was home. With several envelopes in his hands, he opened the door and put them on the table. Then, he took a shower and cooked himself an omelette. Before he sat down and started eating, he turned on the radio.

- *Honolulu, it's Waikiki News reporter Liz Anderson! Today, the whole city is shocked by the sudden death of a local businessman, Gilbert Frederich. With Detective Gerald Horwitz by my side, I'm going to ask him some questions!*

Herbie thought to himself.

- Oh, for goodness' sake!

- *So Gerald, tell me about yourself.*
- *Well, Liz, I'm just a warrior against crime! That murderer doesn't stand a chance when I'm on the scene!*

The reporter laughed.

- *Wow, Gerald! You sound really confident about yourself!*
- *Come on, Liz. I'm just doing my job! Stop flirting with me!*

The reporter laughed again.

Herbie got annoyed and turned off the radio.

- Gee! Finally!

When he finished his omelette, he started opening the envelopes. In one of the envelopes, there was a letter. Herbie began reading.

- *Dear Father,*

  It's me, Philip, your son! I haven't heard from you for so long! I wanted to say how sorry I am for everything I've done. I know I wasn't a good son. It's been too long. You probably won't believe me but I miss you. I miss you very much. My life in France is good these days. This place is different from America but I like it. It's been hard during the war, though. I had to jointhe army, too. Luckily, I survived and kept my family safe. Judith and I got married! We have two children! One of them is a little girl called Julia and the other one is Inés! You know, Inés is a common name in France. Julia is six and Inés is two! That's right! You've been a grandfather for a few years already! I'm so sorry, Dad. I thought of writing to you much earlier but I just couldn't find the courage after all I've done to you. Maybe you've wanted to do the same but you didn't have my address. Dad, I wanted to ask you something. We have enough money to come to Hawaii now. It'll be Christmas soon and I would like to spend it with you! Please,Father, forgive me. I'll understand ifyou don't think it's a good idea. Just please, write me a letter.

Sincerely yours,

Philip.

P.S. How's your work?

Herbie was shocked. His thoughts scattered in his mind.

- This is unbelievable! Philip! He's alive! I'm a grandfather and I didn't even know about it! I have to write him!

He stood up from the chair and grabbed his pen and a piece of paper. After a little while, he took a deep breath and started writing.

- *Dear Philip,*

I simply have no words regarding your letter. I'm still shocked by the things I've just read from you. After so many years, you have decided to get in touch with your father. First, I want to tell you something, son. I love you! No matter what happened between us, you will always be my son. Second, I understand your lack of courage to get in touch with me before, but son... You should have written me a letter the day I became a grandfather! It was very impolite of you to keep something like this a secret for so long! What would your poor mother think if she found out about this? Anyway, I'm really glad that you wrote me. Seriously, I thought you were dead, son! About your offer for a Christmas visit, you're welcome to come here! I haven't heard from your brother and sister for a while now. Nevertheless, it's still a very nice thought spending Christmas with my family once again!

Love,

Herbie (your dad, in case you forgot my name).

P.S. My work is fine. I'm currently investigating the murder of a famous local businessman, Gilbert Frederich. You have probably heard about it in the news.

Herbie read the letter once more with his hands shaking.Finally, he put it in the envelope. He wrote Philip's address by looking at the envelope in which he had sent his letter. A few minutes later, Herbie went to the post office and sent the letter. Even though he felt slightly miserable after so much news from Philip, he also felt happy for what had happened.

A few hours passed and Herbie was at home relaxing. After another few hours, he went to bed.

VII.

The Police Station
4 December, 1947

It was ten o'clock in the morning when Herbie arrived at the police station. As he was walking down the corridor, he met Gerald.

- Horwitz! Fine, you're here already! Let's go to the lieutenant's office.

Gerald replied.

- Ok, Herbie.

They both went to the office. Lieutenant More was sitting in his chair waiting for them.

- Fox! Horwitz! How's the investigation going? Any progress?

Herbie replied.

- Yes, Lieutenant. We interrogated Gilbert Frederich's wife, Claudia and his business partner, Joe Pentham.
- Good, Fox. Are you two getting along well?

This time, Gerald replied.

- Yes, Lieutenant. We're like brothers already. If Herbie was Mozart, I would be... uh... Mozart's songwriting partner?

Herbie and the lieutenant looked annoyingly at Gerald. A few seconds later, Herbie added his two cents.

- As you can see, Lieutenant, Gerald is still acting like a child.

Lieutenant responded with an angry look on his face.

- I see that. Fox, could you please leave us alone for a minute? Don't worry, it won't be long.

Herbie went out of the office. He sat down on a chair in the corridor and waited. Meanwhile, he heard the lieutenant's shouting. He thought to himself.

- Hmm... sounds like he's in trouble.

After a few moments, Gerald fiercely opened the door and shouted.

- Great! My work here is done!

Herbie was surprised and went to the office. Lieutenant More was very angry. With a burst of anger, he told Herbie in sorrow.

- Fox! I'm sorry but... I'm really not feeling well. This is just too much for me! I've decided that Horwitz is no longer your partner.

Herbie surprise grew. He felt angry but also confused.

- What do you mean, Lieutenant?

While the lieutenant was grabbing a bottle of scotch, he replied.

- You heard me, Fox. Forget about Horwitz! You're on your own from now on!

Herbie didn't know what to say. In confusion, he tried to persuade the lieutenant.

- Lieutenant, I don't know if this is a smart decision. It's true that I prefer to work alone on things but this case is just too serious. Horwitz may not be that well-mannered but he helped me out a little yesterday. If he wasn't with me at the crime scene, I would have been surrounded by journalists!

Lieutenant stated in a bigger anger than before.

- Don't be so stressed out, Fox! That guy is an idiot! Believe me, it'll be better without him! Just try it out, will you?

Herbie replied with insecurity.

- I'm still not sure about this, Lieutenant.
- Come on, Fox! You'll be fine! Just go!

Herbie sighed and responded.

- All right, Lieutenant. I guess you know what you're doing. Take care.

Herbie left the office and went out of the building. When he got in the car, he thought to himself.

- Gee, am I really supposed to drive now? Let's see, where should I go?

He looked at his notebook.

- Hmm... Claudia Frederich stated that Gilbert liked to hang out in the Lopez Hills Bar. I'll trythere, I suppose.

Herbie started the car and drove to the Lopez Hills Bar. When he got inside, there was a middle-aged barkeeper behind the counter. He was an obese man with short black hair. Herbiewas uncomfortable because he recognised him. They had had a rough argument on Herbie's last visit.When the barkeeper saw Herbie, he shouted.

- Hey! It's you again! You're that lousy detective from a few months ago! What do you want?

Herbie approached the bar and spoke to the barkeeper.

- I have a few questions for you, my beloved barkeeper.

The barkeeper was surprised and replied with a smile on his face.

- Are you investigating some murder again? I swear, you're probably the only man in this town who never comes to drink here. At your age, that is. Come on, let me serve you a glass of fine scotch! I'll answer your questions. This one is on me!

Herbie wanted to refuse the barkeeper's offer but when he saw the bottle of scotch, he couldn't seem to resist. He was surprised by the kind offer, too.

- Well, I have to calm down a little, anyway. All right then, you can do that!

The barkeeper served Herbie a drink and gave him the glass.

- Here you are, fella. So what do you want this time?

Herbie sipped the drink and replied.

- Have you heard about the murder of Gilbert Frederich?

The barkeeper thought for a minute and responded.

- Yes. Oh, I see where this is going. You're correct, he was here two days ago.

Herbie was surprised and sipped for the second time.

- Really? Come on, tell me. What was he doing here?

The barkeeper laughed.

- What are you doing here right now, detective? He came here to get drunk, just like everyone else!

Herbie laughed quietly and stated with a smile. He sipped the drink for the third time.

- You're right! You know what? Give me another glass! I like this!

The barkeeper served another drink of scotch to Herbie. When he gave it to, he told him.

- Here you are, detective. This one is on you, though.

Herbie started to look angry and claimed.

- All right, all right, my barkeeper, just give it to me!

Herbie finished the first glass and started drinking from the next one. Afterwards, he finally started asking further questions about Gilbert's visit.

- What did Gilbert Frederich tell you when he was here?

The barkeeper replied.

- That guy was miserable. He complained about a lot of things. About his company's bankruptcy, about his wife, he whined a lot about his friend. He also complained about some lousy breakfast his wife served him that morning. He said it made him throw up several times that day. Afterwards, he got drunk and before I knew it, he was gone.

Herbie grew curious.

- What did he say about his wife?

The barkeeper thought for a minute and answered the question.

- Let me see. Yes... he complained about their marriage. He said they were arguing a lot and he was thinking about a divorce.

Herbie was surprised and stated.

- You have to be kidding me! What else did he say?

The barkeeper continued.

- He complained about how they couldn't have any kids.

Herbie was shocked. He finished the second glass and shouted. His signs of intoxication were apparent.

- Unbelievable! Now, give me another drink!

The barkeeper wondered about Herbie.

- Really, detective? Another one? You're beginning to look like an Irishman, fella!

Herbie became irritated.

- Oh, come on, my beloved barkeeper! I want to drink! These glasses look empty!

The barkeeper served Herbie another drink. Meanwhile, Gerald came into the bar. When he saw Herbie, he shouted.

- Whoa! Herbie man! Good to see you here, man! Bartender, give me a nice glass of dry Martini!

The barkeeper was curious.

- You two know each other?

Gerald replied.

- You bet! We are warriors against crime! Ain't that right, Herbie?

Herbie laid his head on the counter,feelingexhausted. He just mumbled.

- Mmm...

Gerald told the barkeeper.

- You see! He confirmed it!

The barkeeper shook his head softly and stated.

- Two detectives drinking on the job... That's quite sad.

Gerald became angry and replied.

- Whoa, whoa, whoa, bartender! You have a problem with that? Say that to my face!

Herbie woke up for a moment. When he saw Gerald shouting at the barkeeper, he tried to fall asleep again. Gerald continued.

- Pal, say a word about me or Herbie, here, and we'll kick your ass!

The barkeeper started shouting, too.

- You want to go outside? Okay! Let's fight, you two chumps!

Gerald shouted at Herbie. He tried to wake him up.

- Herbie! Wake up! We're going to rumble! Herbie! Come on, rascal!

The barkeeper laughed and stated.

- He ain't gonna help you, pal! Don't be a wuss! Let's go!

Gerald and the barkeeper went outside and started fighting. A few moments later, Herbie woke up and began to feel much better. When he saw the fight, he was surprised.

- What... what happened here? Horwitz? Oh no...

Suddenly, one of the people in the bar approached Herbie.

- Mister Fox? May I speak with you for a moment?

Herbie replied.

- Of course. What would you like to tell me?

The man continued. He was a young, skinny-looking man with round glasses and short brown hair.

- I've heard that you're investigating the murder of Gilbert Frederich. I was here two days ago. I can give you some information.

Herbie smiled and responded.

- That's good news! You can start.

The man started explaining.

- My name is John Hawkeye. I was here before Gilbert Frederich's arrival. When he entered the bar, he looked devastated. He ordered a glass of vodka and soon after, he was ordering more and more glasses. He complained a lot about his spouse,Claudia.

Herbie interrupted John's testimony.

- Yes, the barkeeper told me that already just a few minutes ago. What did he say about his friend Joe?

John continued.

- He felt angry with him. He wondered how his business went bankrupt without him doing anything about it.

Herbie thought for a minute.

- Interesting. Did something happen when he was here?

John replied.

- Actually, yes. He got into a fight with the barkeeper, just like your friend here now.

Herbie was surprised.

- You have to be kidding me! How did that happen?

John explained.

- The thing was, Gilbert was drinking a lot two days ago. When he had to pay, he wanted to put it on his tab. The barkeeper refused to do that. Gilbert tried to explain that he lost all his money but the barkeeper didn't believe him. A moment later, the barkeeper asked Gilbert to go outside with him. It looks like he beat him up pretty bad. The strange thing was, it took about twenty minutes before the barkeeper returned. Gilbert wasn't with him anymore.

After a short moment, Gerald and the barkeeper returned. Herbie stood up from his chair and declared.

- Barkeeper! You're under arrest!

Gerald laughed out loud and the barkeeper looked shocked.

- Are you serious, you fat lump? What for?

Herbie replied.

- I've just received information about what really happened here two days ago. You have some explaining to do at the police station! Horwitz! Here are the cuffs. Get him in the car! You're driving to the station. I don't feel so well.

Gerald took the cuffs and used them on the barkeeper. Then, he put him in the police car. Herbie came along soon after and sat in the passenger's seat. During the commute to the police station, the barkeeper grew nervous and started talking.

- Do you know what you're doing, you two suckers? This is not a smart move!

Gerald responded. Herbie wasn't feeling good and he had a strong headache. He tried to remain silent the entire time.

- Don't think you're going to get away with this, bartender! Herbie here is one of the greatest in this town! He knows exactly why you're going to the police station!

The barkeeper tried to threaten Herbie.

- You! Herbie guy! When this is over, you'll regret this!

Herbie felt tired again. He tried to calm down the barkeeper with a softer voice than usual.

- Don't try to threaten me, barkeeper! The testimony was clear! You beat up Gilbert Frederich! We'll just have a little talk at the police station. No one has accused you yet. If you are not the murderer, you can relax.

The barkeeper was still nervous. A few minutes later, they reached the police station. Gerald was leading the barkeeper inside and Herbie was walking besides them. In the corridor, the lieutenant saw them and spoke to Herbie.

- Fox! What is Horwitz doing here? I gave you a clear statement that you're on your own now!

Herbie responded.

- Lieutenant, he's just helping me out with a suspect. I met him by coincidence in Lopez Hills Bar. I probably wouldn't be able to carry him here by myself. I'm experiencing a strong headache right now.

Lieutenant nodded softly and asked further questions.

- All right, Fox. Who is the suspect?

Herbie replied.

- The barkeeper. One of the customers gave a testimony about him. He beat up Gilbert Frederich the night he was murdered!

Lieutenant stated.

- I see. I'll go with you to interrogate him now. Let's put him in interrogation room three.
-

Herbie shouted at Gerald.

- Horwitz! Put him in interrogation room three! We can start the questioning!

After a while, Herbie and the lieutenant went to the interrogation room. Gerald sat the barkeeper at the table and Herbie sat down. Herbie opened his notebook and grabbed his pen. He started talking.

- All right. We can start the interrogation. Did you have any relationship with Gilbert Frederich? Were you two friends?

The barkeeper replied in fury.

- Don't think I'll come off easy, detective! I want my lawyer before saying anything to you! You're not the only one who can play rough!

Lieutenant More started shouting.

- Speak or we'll put you in jail! Don't think you can play with us!

The barkeeper calmed down slightly and responded.

- Ok, ok, chump!

Lieutenant More replied immediately.

- Lieutenant More to you! You're going to treat me with respect, you lowlife!

The barkeeper responded.

- Gee! Ok, Lieutenant. I was Frederich's client. The bar costs me a lot to maintain. That's why I had to apply for a cash loan. I'm not proud of it. Unfortunately, I had no other option.

Herbie was surprised and stated.

- That's good, actually! Tell me about Calico. It's been said that Sunbeam Finances had no clients left when they went bankrupt. Could you give us some insight into this situation?

The barkeeper replied.

- Yes... I can. Just a few days ago, I started receiving letters from Calico. In those letters, they were trying to persuade me to switch from Sunbeam Finances to them. They promised me a ⊠revolutionary plan".

Herbie was curious.

- What was this ⏹revolutionary plan" supposed to be?

The barkeeper answered the question.

- Much lower fees, no extra charges for switching from Sunbeam Finances, no hassle with the corporates, they even wanted to pay one payment for me. It seemed like a fairy tale to me.

Herbie asked further.

- Did you accept their offer?

The barkeeper hesitated about what to say for a moment.

- Well, unfortunately for me... no.

Herbie was curious about the barkeeper's answer.

- What happened to you? Why was it unfortunate?

The barkeeper replied.

- When Gilbert was in the bar... he told me about some unfortunate things.

Herbie became slightly angry.

- What unfortunate things? Come on, just say it!

The barkeeper continued.

- He told me that I have a debt. All the money he loaned me became his debt. I didn't understand clearly what he was trying to explain to me. All I knew was... that I'm screwed and I have a huge debt. I might even have to shut down my bar!

Herbie was surprised and something came up in his mind.

- So... that's why you beat him up? What was your reaction to this statement?

The barkeeper replied.

- I was shocked... I became miserable. How was I supposed to react? I wanted to cry... Are you happy now, detectives? The reason why I fought him was... he had about twenty expensive drinks. He couldn't pay for them and he wanted to put it on his tab. I got so mad that I couldn't stand the pressure anymore. He put my whole family into debt. Then he made me another one by not paying. I admit... I told him to come outside with me and I beat him up like a bag of potatoes.

Herbie responded.

- I see. The witness told me that it took you about twenty minutes to come back to the bar. Also, Gilbert was nowhere to be seen. How come?

The barkeeper grew frightened and tried to explain.

- I... We... We were just talking things out for quite a long time. When I punched him, that bastard tried to persuade me how sorry he was for what he had caused me. He cried like a baby. I tried to calm him down. I couldn't just leave him like that.

Herbie was suspicious.

- Something's just not quite right, barkeeper. I'm sorry but... I think you'll spend some time in a prison cell tonight. We need more information before we can let you go.

The barkeeper grew very angry and shouted.

- That's ridiculous! I'm innocent, you bastards! You can't throw me in jail! I have a family and they need me!

Herbie tried to calm the barkeeper down.

- Listen, calm down! You won't spend a long time here if you're really innocent. We just need to verify your testimony with the testimonies of others!

Then Herbie shouted.

- Officer Blake! Come here!

Officer Blake entered the room and spoke to Herbie.

- What can I do for you, detective?

Herbie pointed at the barkeeper and replied.

- You know what to do, officer.

Herbie left the room. Gerald followed him.

- Hey, Herbie! You looked so tough in there!

Herbie kept walking and remained silent. Gerald continued.

- Hey! Herbie! What are you going to do now? Let's get some other punk into jail! Ain't that right? Come on, Herbie! Talk to me!

Herbie replied to Gerald with frustration.

- Look, Horwitz! Thank you for all your help but we're finished. You're not my partner anymore!

Gerald responded.

- But Herbie! We're a great team! You don't need the lieutenant's approval! You know that well! What would you have done without me in that bar? Admit it, we get along well in this job!

Herbie got a little upset and stated.

- Horwitz, maybe you're right... Look, rules are rules. You're not in the game anymore. I'm sorry... This is purely my case now.

Gerald tried to pursuade Herbie a bit more.

- Herbie! Come on! Just think about it, please! I need this job! My family needs it! Talk to the lieutenant. I beg you!

Herbie thought for a little while and replied.

- Well... Horwitz. All right. I'll see what I can do about it. I've tried it already, to be honest with you.

Gerald stated.

- Thank you, Herbie. You don't know how much it means to me!

Herbie responded.

- I haven't promised you anything, Horwitz. Just leave everything up to me.

Herbie left the building and accessed the nearest telephone booth. He spoke into the receiver.

- Operator, I need an address! Detective Herbie Fox.

After a little while, a female voice answered.

- This is the operator! Who is the person, detective?

Herbie replied.

- Martin Kipp. Owner of the Calico company.
- Just a minute, detective.

After about a minute, Herbie received the address and got into his car.

VIII.

Martin Kipp
4 December, 1947

A few minutes later, Herbie arrived at Martin Kipp's house. It was a massive villa with a large garden and a fountain placed in front of the door. Herbie couldn't believe his eyes and thought to himself.

- My goodness! I haven't seen such a big house in a very long time.

When arrived at the door, he rang the doorbell. It played a little tune. After a short moment, a female maid opened the door. She spoke to Herbie.

- Si? I mean yes, sir?

Herbie responded.

- Detective Herbie Fox. Is Martin Kipp home, Miss?

The maid replied.

- Si... I mean yes. Come inside.

She led Herbie to the living room and stated.

- Sit down, detective. I go and talk to Sir Kipp.

Herbie replied with a smile.

- All right, Miss. Thank you kindly.

Herbie sat down on the sofa. The maid went upstairs and Herbie heard her knocking on a door, The door opened and he heard her speaking.

- Mister Kipp, some detective is here. He want talk to you.

Martin responded in a terrified tone of voice.

- What? Come here for a minute!

The maid went inside the room and Martin closed the door. Afterwards, Herbie heard a glass breaking and indistinguishable shouting. A little while later, Martin came down the stairs. He was a middle-aged man with short brown hair and a thin figure. He wore a blue sweater and black trousers. As he was coming down the stairs, he spoke to Herbie.

- Mister Fox! Glad to meet you!

Herbie stood up as Martin approached him and they shook hands. Martin continued talking.

- It's a pleasure to meet you, Mister Fox. I know why you're here, to be honest. I've been expecting you.

Herbie replied.

- Good to know, Mister Kipp. Without further ado, let's start.

Herbie opened his notebook and grabbed his pen. The maid brought a cup of tea.

- Have some tea! Very good, lemon tea!

Suddenly, Martin shouted.

- Thalia, for goodness' sake! Can't you see we're having a serious conversation here?

Herbie was surprised and stated.

- It's all right, Mister Kipp. I would love to have a cup of tea, Miss Thalia!

Thalia looked happy when she heard Herbie's words. Herbie took a cup of tea and sipped it. Then, he continued the conversation with Martin.

- Mister Kipp. Let's begin then. Tell me about your relationship with Gilbert Frederich. Did you two know each other?

Martin smiled and replied.

- Of course. I can't say we were friends, though. We met a few times on various occasions and that was pretty much it.

Herbie asked further.

- What about his business partner, Joe Pentham?

Martin answered the question.

- Joe... now that's a whole different story! We're good friends! Honestly, that man is on his sure way to the top!

Herbie was curious.

- What do you mean by that?

Martin responded.

- He's a powerful and solid businessman. I see a lot of potential in that guy! I even loaned him some money so he could start his car company, Ride-O-Mobil!

Herbie was surprised.

-   Is that so?

Martin replied.

-   Yes. I've seen the reports. No regrets!

Herbie continued asking questions.

-   That's odd. I have some more serious questions for you now. Tell me about your company, Calico. How did it start out?

Martin grew a little frightened and started explaining.

-   It's a business I started just a few months ago. We provide cash loan services. It all started when a good friend of mine complained about Sunbeam Finances.

Herbie thought for a minute.

-   Really? Who was that friend of yours?

Martin got nervous and tried to change the topic of the conversation.

-   That's not important, detective. Let's move on, shall we?

Herbie grew suspicious immediately.

-   Why can't you tell me, Mister Kipp? Was it Joe? Don't lie to me, Mister Kipp!

Martin got very frightened and responded.

-   Yes... I mean no! Ok, it was him.

Herbie started raising his voice slightly.

-   What did he complain about, Mister Kipp?

Martin remained silent for a short moment. Herbie stated.

-   Tell me, Mister Kipp. You don't have to hide anything from me. Either you tell the truth or I'll find out another way, and in that case, it'll be worse for you!

Martin broke down.

-   All right, all right, detective! I'll tell you everything! Joe complained about Gilbert. All the time! He thought it wasn't fair that Gilbert was the boss and not him! He said that Gilbert wasn't responsible enough to lead such a powerful company. You know, Joe always wanted to be the boss. Gilbert didn't let him havethat position. Never! I'm about to tell you something very confidental now.

Herbie was curious.

- What is it, Mister Kipp?

Martin took a deep breath.

- One day, Joe called me. He wanted me to...

Martin seemed to be too afraid to finish the sentence. Herbie pushed him into it.

- Come on, Mister Kipp. You can do it! Finish the sentence, please.

Martin took another deep breath.

- He wanted me to hire a gunman for him. He asked me to... kill Gilbert.

Herbie was shocked and shouted.

- You... you just can't be serious! What a scumbag!

Herbie stood up, intending to call the police to arrest Joe. Martin stopped him.

- Please don't do that, Mister Fox! It was a long time ago! Joe got over the fact that he couldn't be the boss of Sunbeam Finances soon after that incident!

Herbie hesitated but agreed. He realised that the interrogation was not over yet. He stated.

- All right, Mister Kipp. Let's finish this interrogation before making any assumptions.

Herbie sat down again and the conversation continued.

- Mister Kipp, there is one thing that really concerns me about Calico. How is it possible that it took over all of Sunbeam Finances clients?

Martin smiled and replied.

- I guess you can ask that question of our clients, Mister Fox. I don't know why they decided to switch to our company. Our only strategy was to build a fair marketing plan to inform the citizens of Honolulu about us. Nothing that special about it.

Herbie thought for a minute about the statement. He continued asking questions.

- What about the clients who didn't switch to your company? I have testimony from one person about the situation. He stated that he didn't switch from Sunbeam Finances to your company and that caused him a huge debt. Can you say something about that, Mister Kipp?

Martin thought about it. After a short moment, he stated.

- No, I can't, Mister Fox. This is quite surprising for me to hear. I thought that all of their clients switched to Calico. In any case, it sounds reasonable. If someone didn't make the switch before the bankruptcy occured, he suddenly carrys the company's troubles on his shoulders. How could a bankrupt company loan someone money? Think about it. Can you give me some contact information for the unfortunate person? We can help him pay off the debt.

Herbie responded.

- That's very kind of you, Mister Kipp. I'll let you know when that person turns out to be innocent. It doesn't look good for him at this moment. Let's move on now. What can you tell me about Gilbert's wife Claudia? Do you know her?

Martin replied.

- Just as much as I knew Gilbert. Maybe even less, actually. Gilbert introduced us at one of the events we both attended. She's a beautiful lady, I have to say. We had a little conversation and that was all. Surprisingly, she told me about her problems with Gilbert. She was thinking of divorcing him at that time.

Herbie was surprised and stated.

- That woman told everyone the truth except me! Why would that be?

Herbie started thinking. Martin responded.

- It's not surprising, Mister Fox. Have you heard any of the radio shows she appeared on? When asked in public, she always lied about her marriage with Gilbert. If anyone asked her a question concerning Gilbert, he was the best man alive and she was the happiest woman on Earth to be his wife. Actually, I can prove it to you! I have a vinyl record of one of her radio interviews! Hawaii Flash Radio had a special sale one day. They were selling various recordings of their shows. Just a moment, I'll set up the phono cartridge and bring the record.

Martin set up his phono cartridge and turned it on. Afterwards, he opened one of his wardrobes and pulled out the recording. He placed it on the cartridge and played it.

- *Greetings to our fellow listeners. You're listening to Hawaii Talk. My name is Sam Turkins and I'll be your host for today's episode. Our special guest today is the spouse of famous local businessman Gilbert Frederich, owner of a trending company called Sunbeam Finances. Please welcome Claudia Frederich!*

Claudia spoke.

- *Good evening to you, Sam. I'm pleased to be on theshow.*

Sam started the conversation.

- *Claudia, you're such a handsome young woman. How does it feel to be married to such a powerful man of our town?*
- *It's a lot of joy, Sam. Gilbert is the most wonderful man I've ever met. I love him very much.*
- *That's very nIce to hear, Claudia. It sounds like you're a happy couple. Is that right, Claudia?*
- *Oh, yes it is, Sam. We're currently thinking about having children.*
- *That's interesting, Claudia. Anyway, tell us something about yourself. What are your hobbies, for instance?*
- *I like playing tennis and I have a lot of passion for art.*

- *Yes, it is known that you're not too shabby a painter, Claudia. One of your paintings hasjust been presented in the National Gallery, is that correct?*
- *Yes, Sam. I'm very proud that one of my works reached the National Gallery. It's a great honor for me.*
- *What did Gilbert say about your paintings?*
- *Honestly, he doesn't like them very much. I'm just kidding, he loves them! He was very happy when I told him about the presentation of my paintings at the gallery.*
- *Wonderful, Claudia. How long have you been playing tennis?*
- *I've played tennis for many years now. Gilbert even bought me my own tennis court. He's such a caring man.*

Martin stopped the vinyl recording.

- I think I have proved my point, haven't I?

Herbie replied.

- Yes, you have. That's quite interesting, I have to say. Needless to say, I'm probably not wondering that much about it. Gilbert Frederich was really quite a popular man here.

Herbie stood up from the sofa and continued.

- All right, Mister Kipp. I think we're done. You're a fine man, Mister Kipp.

Martin smiled and responded.

- I have the same thoughts about you, Mister Fox. Thank you for your visit.

Herbie stated.

- Take care, Mister Kipp.

Herbie left Martin's house. When he was gone, Martin picked up his telephone and dialed Joe's number. After a short while, Joe answered and Martin told him in a stressed tone of voice.

- Joe! Joe! I've just had a visit.

Joe asked in confusion.

- A visit? From whom?

Martin replied.

- It was a detective Herbie Fox. Listen, I don't know how to say this. I have no idea why but he thinks you're the murderer. He was talking about you the whole time!

Joe was frightened.

- Me? That's ridiculous. Have you talked with Claudia about it yet? She will lose her mind! I can't go to jail just because some detective thinks I'm a murderer!

Martin answered.

- No, should I? Hang on! Has she found out anything about the will yet?

Joe grew excited and replied.

- Surprisingly, yes! It may be better than we thought it was at first!

Martin replied.

- That sounds good. You should try to run now, though. That detective will be at your house soon!

Joe responded.

- Ok, Martin. Thanks for calling me. Bye.

Martin hung up the telephone.

IX.

Joe Pentham
4 December, 1947

Herbie was driving a police car. He called dispatch to arrest Joe.

- Dispatch! This is Herbie Fox! I need police backup to arrest a suspect named Joe Pentham. The address is 449 Lanipuao Street.

A female voice spoke from the transmitter.

- All right, detective. Sending police backup to 449 Lanipuao Street.

A few minutes later, Herbie arrived at Joe's house. The police backup was there already. When Joe opened the door and saw the policemen, he tried to rush to his car and escape them. His attempt was not successful. Joe was arrested and brought to the police station. Herbie started the interrogation in interrogation room two. Lieutenant More was in the room, too.

- Joe Pentham! I think you remember me. I have some serious questions for you this time! I have testimony which says you attempted to hire a gunman to kill

Gilbert Frederich in the past. What can you tell us about that, Joe?

Joe was frightened. He replied.

- I have no idea what you're talking about! I've never wanted to hire a gunman to kill Gilbert! He was my good friend!

Herbie shouted.

- Don't lie to me, Joe! I know that you've always wanted to be the leader of Sunbeam Finances! Gilbert never gave you a chance and you were frustrated!

Joe was very nervous and tried to persuade Herbie further.

- Yes, that's true, detective! I've always thought that Gilbert was not responsible enough to lead such a huge company. I would never want to kill him, though! I started my own company just a few months ago! I didn't feel the need to be the boss of Sunbeam Finances anymore!

Herbie thought for a minute. Afterwards, he asked further.

- All right, Joe. Let's say I believe you. Tell me now. What is your relationship with Claudia Frederich?

Joe answered the question in great fear.

- We are just friends! I swear!

Herbie was very suspicious. He shouted once again.

- I think you're a pretty big liar, Joe! No! It doesn't seem like the correct answer to me! Officer Blake, go out and bring Claudia Frederich here!

Officer Blake responded.

- Yes, Mister Fox. Just give me a few minutes.

Officer Blake went out of the building and drove to Claudia's house. Meanwhile, Herbie was trying to push Joe even more.

- Joe! I have a feeling that you have kept many secrets from me! Giving a false testimony is a federal crime! Do you realise that? If Claudia Frederich says something different than you, you'll be punished! It doesn't matter if you're innocent or not! Joe, I advise you to tell me truth before Claudia arrives! Come on!

Joe panicked and broke down. He started explaining.

- All right, detective! Do you want the truth? I'll tell you the truth! Claudia and I are lovers! She's wanted to divorce Gilbert for years! Their marriage wasn't happy at all!

Herbie was surprised and asked further.

- I should have thought so! How long have you been lovers?

Joe replied.

- It may be two years. And yes, it is true that I wanted to hire a gunman on Gilbert once! That man was miserable! If he had died back then, I would have been the boss of Sunbeam Finances! It's all gone now! That company is ruined to the core! Claudia thought the same about Gilbert. In fact, she hated Gilbert! She may seem like an innocent and tender woman but she's a devil in disguise!

Herbie wanted to ask more but Dean Marston interrupted the negotation. He entered the room and spoke to Herbie.

- Mister Fox! Good, you're here! You have to come with me! I have a shocking discovery for you!

Herbie responded.

- Yes, Mister Marston. I'm coming!

Herbie left the interrogation room. He went to the laboratory room with Dean where Dean revealed the body of Gilbert Frederich. He started explaining.

- Mister Fox! This was probably one of the hardest bodies for me to make observations about! You see, it was unbelievable for me! There were almost no wounds, no blood on the ground, no signs of sharp objects or anything like that! The only wounds are located on the victim's head and the reason for them is clear already. They were caused by the barkeeper you brought in today! I had to inspect the body further. Look, I found this in the victim's body!

Dean grabbed a small plastic bag with a couple of drops of a dense substance in it. Herbie was curious.

- What is it, Mister Marston?

Dean replied with confidence.

- It's honey! I know what you're thinking. You see, it's not ordinary honey! Not even by a mile! It contains particles originating from rhododendrens, azaleas and oleanders! Mister Fox... this is a deadly poison for the human body! That's our answer! The victim was poisoned! This honey takes about six hours to work. The victim probably consumed it in the morning!

That's why there are no serious wounds, no signs of blunt objects or a drop of blood!

Herbie was surprised. After a minute, he claimed.

-   So the murderer was... Claudia! She... she betrayed her husband! It makes sense! Thank you very much, Mister Marston. I need to go and prove it now. I still don't have enough evidence against her!

Dean stated.

-   How unfortunate! Go, Mister Fox! Make her pay for her sins!

Herbie left the laboratory. In the corridor, there was Claudia being brought to the interrogation room. Herbie returned to the room to finish the interrogation. Claudia and Joe were sitting at the table. Lieutenant More was gone.

-   Well, well, well. Nice to see you, Claudia! I'll get straight to the point. I know about everything, Claudia!

Claudia was surprised and asked with insecurity.

-   About what, detective?

Herbie responded.

- It's over, Claudia! Why did you murder your husband?

Claudia looked shocked.

- I don't know what you're talking about, detective!

Herbie punched the table and shouted very loudly.

- I know about the honey, Claudia! Stop playing games with me! Your lying is over! Why did you do that, Claudia? Why?

Claudia started crying and stated.

- All right, I admit it! I'll tell you! I have something to say about me and Joe!

Joe interrupted Claudia.

- He knows already, Claudia!

Claudia cried even more and continued talking.

- We had a plan together!

Herbie pushed Claudia.

- What plan, Claudia?

Claudia replied.

- The reason why I killed Gilbert was... I found a hidden will of Gilbert's. It promised I would inherit millions of dollars.

Herbie thought for a minute. Something was very unclear to him.

- Wait a minute. Sunbeam Finances was bankrupt! It was stated that Gilbert lost all his money!

Joe tried to explain this time.

- Detective, that was a part of our plan. The truth is... Sunbeam Finances didn't go bankrupt. I found a loophole which meant I was able to shut down the company. I mean... all of the clients taken over by another company? Come on! That doesn't sound real! In fact, Sunbeam Finances was still standing! I saw no point to keep it alive, though. My company Ride-O-Mobil is climbing the ladder every day. Also, Gilbert would never let me be a boss!

Herbie shouted.

- And that's why you had to kill your friend? Because you two were greedy? Shame on you! Tell me about the honey!

Claudia started explaining.

- Joe knew a person who could make poisonous honey. He fed some of his bees on rhododendren plants. All parts of these plants are poisonous. I put it in the cup of tea I gave Gilbert at breakfast. When I heard the news the next morning, a part of me died with Gilbert. I regretted it immediately. I'm sorry to say that you're out of luck, detective... all the honey is gone now. You have no evidence against me!

Herbie responded in anger.

- Don't worry, Claudia! I'll find a way to prove it! I don't know how but I will!

After a short moment of silence, Herbie stated.

- I'm going to the lieutenant's office.

Herbie went to the lieutenant's office. He spoke to the lieutenant.

- Lieutenant! We have the murderer!

Lieutenant was surprised.

- Fox! That's great news! You can start explaining!

Herbie started explaining.

- It's Claudia Frederich, the wife of Gilbert Frederich! She and Joe Pentham had a plan! They wanted to kill Gilbert Frederich because of some hidden will. This will promised Claudia would inherit millions of dollars!

Lieutenant thought about it and wondered.

- But Fox! What about the bankruptcy of Sunbeam Finances?

Herbie replied.

- That's the thing! There was no such bankruptcy of Sunbeam Finances! It was all just a big lie! Joe managed to shut down the company. He told one that the company went bankrupt! He and Claudia probably wanted to make Gilbert Frederich's death look like a suicide!

Lieutenant asked further.

- That sounds interesting, Fox. How did they kill him?

100

Herbie continued.

- The answer is honey. Not a casual honey, though! Joe gave Claudia a special poisonous honey made from bees who were fed on rhododendren plants! It all makes sense! The poison takes six hours to start working! The barkeeper told me that Gilbert complained to him about vomiting several times that day!

Lieutenant smiled and stated.

- Great job, Fox! One last question... where is the evidence?

Herbie got a little upset and replied.

- That's the problem, lieutenant. I... have no evidence. Only those testimonies make this conclusion.

Lieutenant got angry and responded.

- For crying out loud, Fox! How are we supposed to win the court case without any physical evidence? You better find somequick! Do you understand, Fox?

Herbie replied in a lowered tone of voice.

- Yes, Lieutenant.

Suddenly, someone knocked on the door. The door opened and it was Gerald. He was carrying a bag with him. The lieutenant spoke to him.

- Horwitz! What are you doing here! You have no business here! Get out!

Gerald tried to calm down the lieutenant. He was very calm.

- Lieutenant, Herbie, I have something for you.

Gerald opened his bag and Herbie lost his mind when he saw the object. It was a half empty jar with a tag ⬛Honey of Death⬛stuck to it. Gerald explained.

- I found this in Claudia Frederich's house.

Herbie was very excited and asked Gerald.

- Horwitz! My goodness! How... how did you get it?

Gerald replied.

- You know, Herbie, you all think I'm an idiot. I'm not! When we went to visit Claudia Frederich together, I knew there was something going on with that woman. Think about it! She didn't even look upset about the death of her husband! Anyway, after our interrogation with the barkeeper, I did something. I went to visit Claudia Frederich once more. This time, I asked her to make me a cup of tea and I took a look around when she was in the kitchen. Soon, I found this jar in one of the drawers. I simply took it and left. One of my friends is a scientist. I brought him a sample and he confirmed my assumptions. This honey is a deadly poison!

Herbie wanted to cry with joy and he shouted.

-   Horwitz! I don't know what to say! Thanks to you, we can sentence Claudia Frederich! You're a hero!

Gerald laughed and responded.

-   Oh, Herbie! I'm just a warrior against crime, like you! Ain't that right, Herbie?

Herbie smiled and replied.

-   Of course you are, Horwitz! Of course you are!

He turned to the lieutenant.

-   Lieutenant, you have to give this man his job back! You see how much he did for the case in the end!

Gerald remained silent. Lieutenant More thought about it for a moment. After a short while, he stated with insecurity.

- Well, concerning the fact that... Maybe, just maybe... All right. You got me, Fox! Horwitz, here is your badge! Think twice before doing anything stupid, though!

Gerald's eyes filled with happiness. He told the lieutenant.

- Thank you! Thank you so much, Lieutenant! You won't regret this, I swear!

They all three laughed. After a while, Herbie stated seriously.

- Wait just a moment, fellas. I still need to finish something.

Herbie grabbed the jar of honey and went to the interrogation room. He spoke to Claudia and Joe.

- Claudia Frederich, Joe Pentham, you're under arrest for the murder of Gilbert Frederich!

Herbie showed the jar of honey to Claudia and she became terrified. Herbie continued.

- Officer Blake, arrest them!

Officer Blake smiled and replied.

- All right, Mister Fox.

Officer Blake arrested Joe and Claudia. The barkeeper was set free. When Herbie saw him, he spoke to him.

- Barkeeper! My beloved barkeeper! I'm sorry that you had to spend some time in jail.

The barkeeper smiled softly and responded.

- You better be sorry, detective! I told you I'm innocent! Don't you trust me, detective? I served you a free drink, remember? Chump!

They both laughed and Herbie stated.

- Don't worry, barkeeper! We'll get you out of debt! A good friend of mine promised to help you!

The barkeeper was surprised.

- Are you... are you serious, detective?

Herbie replied.

- Yes, yes, my beloved barkeeper! Talk to you soon! I have to go now. Take care!

Herbie returned to the lieutenant's office. Gerald was nowhere to be seen. Herbie took a look outside and there was a group of journalists.

- Mister Horwitz, Liz Anderson speaking. Nice to see you again! So who's the murderer?

Gerald replied with confidence.

- Nice to see you, too, Liz! The warrior against crime has just won the battle!

When Gerald noticed Herbie, he grabbed him and continued.

- What I really meant to say is, the warriors against crime have just won the battle!

Herbie grew uncomfortable and stated.

- Stop it, Horwitz! Seriously!

Gerald laughed and responded.

- Oh, come on, Herbie! Do it for Liz, please!

Herbie smiled and walked away saying.

- I'm telling on you, Horwi lady! Don't make me do that!

Gerald remained silent for a moment. After a little while, he continued.

- Anyway, where were we? Oh yeah, warrior against crime!

Herbie placed his palm on his face.

A few days later, the court sentenced Claudia to fifteen years in prison. Joe was sentenced to ten years in prison for his cooperation. Martin Kipp bought Joe's company, Ride-O-Mobil. Soon after, it became one of the most successful car companies in Honolulu.

X.

Lopez Hills Bar
23 December, 1947

It was eight o'clock in the evening. Herbie was drinking scotch in the Lopez Hills Bar. The barkeeper spoke to him.

- I want to thank you for helping me out with my debt. That Martin Kipp guy is really something! He even paid some of my debt from his own money! What a good man, that chump!

Herbie was feeling very tired and he stated.

- This scotch is good, barkeeper! I can't stop drinking! What have you done? What have you done, barkeeper?

The barkeeper laughed and replied.

- I made your life less miserable, detective! Seriously, if you put me in jail once more, I'll triple the price just for you!

Herbie fell asleep for a few minutes. Afterwards, Herbie came home. At about 11 o'clock in the evening, the doorbell rang. Herbie went to open the door. It was Philip.

- Dad?

Herbie couldn't believe his eyes. He wasvery happy and shouted.

- Philip! You came! You seriously came!

Herbie hugged Philip strongly and tears streamed down his face. Herbie asked him.

- Where's your family, son?

Philip replied.

- They're in a hotel. I wanted to come and see you for at least a little while. Oh, Richard and Veronica are here, too!

Herbie got shocked even more.

- Richard and Veronica? Does this mean that I'm going to spend this year's Christmas with my entire family?

Philip responded.

- I guess so, Dad.

Herbie cried for a little moment. Philip asked him.

-   Are you all right, Dad?

Herbie assured him.

-   Yes, of course I am. I'm just so happy, Son!

The next day, Herbie had a big Christmas dinner with Philip and his family, along with Richard and Veronica, his other children. It was the first time in years thatHerbie was truly happy.

CHARACTERS CHARACTERISTICS

Name: Herbie Fox

Age: 60

Date of Birth: 27/2/1887

Place of Birth: Honolulu, Hawaii

Job: Detective

Family status: Widowed

Children: Philip Fox, Richard Fox, Veronica Fox-Winsley

Appearance: 5 ft 4.96 in, 209 pounds, gray hair, scar on a cheek

Name: Gerald Horwitz

Age: 55

Date of Birth: 20/11/1892

Place of Birth: Honolulu, Hawaii

Job: Detective

Family status: Married

Children: Andrew Horwitz, Margareta Horwitz

Appearance: 6 ft 1.09 in, 180 pounds, black hair

Name: Robert Wintski

Age: 52

Date of Birth: 20/4/1894

Place of Birth: Kapolei, Hawaii

Job: Bartender

Family status: Married

Children: Sylvia Wintski, Thomas Wintski

Appearance: 5 ft 4.17 in, 247 pounds, short black hair

Name: Phil More

Age: 63

Date of Birth: 25/3/1883

Place of Birth: Honolulu, Hawaii

Job: Lieutenant

Family status: Married

Children: George More

Appearance: 5 ft 4 in, 134 pounds, gray hair

Name: Gilbert Frederich

Age: 43

Date of Birth: 9/11/1904

Place of Birth: Honolulu, Hawaii

Job: Businessman

Family status: Married

Children: none

Appearance: 5 ft 6 in, 170 pounds, brown hair, green eyes

Name: Claudia Frederich

Age: 36

Date of Birth: 29/5/1911

Place of Birth: Honolulu, Hawaii

Job: unemployed

Family status: Married

Children: none

Appearance: 5 ft 8 in, 110 pounds, black hair, blue eyes

Name: Joe Pentham

Age: 42

Date of Birth: 30/7/1905

Place of Birth: Honolulu, Hawaii

Job: Businessman

Family status: Single

Children: none

Appearance: 5 ft 7 in, 157 pounds, black hair

Name: Martin Kipp

Age: 35

Date of Birth: 12/9/1912

Place of Birth: Honolulu, Hawaii

Job: Businessman

Family status: Single

Children: none

Appearance: 5 ft 9 in, 145 pounds, short brown hair

About The Author

Steven Vagovics is a young author from Slovakia. Besides writing, Vagovics showed high interest in music. In 2013, he released an EP album on his own which contained five songs recorded at his home. The album was available for a free download on his website. His LP album is about to be released sometime in 2015. In 2010, he created a YouTube account where he regularly posts his stereo mixes and remasters of the songs by The Beatles. Written in 2014, 'The Mystery of Bloody River' is Steven's second book in the established 'Herbie Fox Stories' series. Steven Vagovics received several awards throughout his elementary school years in English competitions.

ALSO AVAILABLE

Check out these other titles in the 'Herbie Fox Stories' series.

Audiobook available soon!

www.ingramcontent.com/pod-product-compliance
Lightning Source LLC
Chambersburg PA
CBHW020150180626
46810CB00004B/1815